Legends, Myths, and Folktales

Celebrate the stories that have moved the world for centuries

ENCYCLOPÆDIA
Britannica®

CHICAGO   LONDON   NEW DELHI   PARIS   SEOUL   SYDNEY   TAIPEI   TOKYO

© 2003 BY ENCYCLOPÆDIA BRITANNICA, INC.

International Standard Book Number: 1-59339-037-8

No part of this work may be reproduced or utilized in any form or by any means, electronic or mechanical, including photocopying, recording, or by any information storage and retrieval system, without permission in writing from the publisher.

BRITANNICA LEARNING LIBRARY: LEGENDS, MYTHS, AND FOLKTALES 2003

Britannica.com may be accessed on the Internet at http://www.britannica.com.

(Trademark Reg. U.S. Pat. Off.) Printed in U.S.A.

Legends, Myths, and Folktales

INTRODUCTION

What was Excalibur?

Who stabbed a one-eyed man-eating giant? Where do Jataka tales come from?

Was the 'Trojan horse' *really* a horse?

In *Legends, Myths, and Folktales,* you'll discover answers to these questions and many more. Through pictures, articles, stories, and fun facts, you'll learn about the exciting, magical tales that have entertained us for centuries, taught us right from wrong, and explained the many mysteries of the world.

To help you on your journey, we've provided the following signposts in *Legends, Myths, and Folktales*:

■ **Subject Tabs**—The coloured box in the upper corner of each right-hand page will quickly tell you the article subject.

■ **Search Lights**—Try these mini-quizzes before and after you read the article and see how much - *and how quickly* - you can learn. You can even make this a game with a reading partner. (Answers are upside down at the bottom of one of the pages.)

■ **Did You Know?**—Check out these fun facts about the article subject. With these surprising 'factoids', you can entertain your friends, impress your teachers, and amaze your parents.

■ **Picture Captions**—Read the captions that go with the photos. They provide useful information about the article subject.

■ **Vocabulary**—New or difficult words are in **bold type**. You'll find them explained in the Glossary at the end of the book.

■ **Learn More!**—Follow these pointers to related articles in the book. These articles are listed in the Table of Contents and appear on the Subject Tabs.

Britannica
LEARNING LIBRARY

Have a great trip!

Legends, Myths, and Folktales

TABLE OF CONTENTS

Stories of Wonders
and Everyday Life

SEARCH LIGHT

Which of the following is a story about ordinary people doing unusual things?
a) myth
b) fable
c) folktale

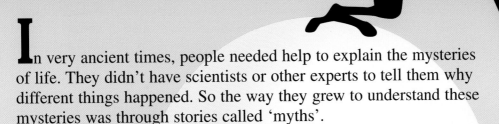

In very ancient times, people needed help to explain the mysteries of life. They didn't have scientists or other experts to tell them why different things happened. So the way they grew to understand these mysteries was through stories called 'myths'.

Today when we call something a myth, we usually mean that it isn't true. But that's often because we don't believe the very old stories. People used to believe in myths very strongly.

Some of the most familiar European myths come from ancient Greece. The gods and goddesses of Greek religion all had stories about them that explained just why things were the way they were.

World religions today have their own mythologies. Hinduism, for example, is filled with wondrous tales of gods and heroes, such as the elephant-headed god Ganesha, who represents good luck. One Bible story tells how Moses led the original Jews out of slavery in Egypt. And the famous stories of Jesus stand as examples to Christians of a perfect life.

Myths are closely related to several other kinds of stories that teach us lessons. These include folktales, legends, fables, and fairy tales.

Folktales are very much like myths, though they are usually about ordinary characters in unusual situations.

Legends resemble folktales and myths, but they're usually linked to a particular place or person that is real or imaginary.

Fables teach lessons by telling stories with animal characters.

Fairy tales sometimes carry a message about right and wrong. But often they're simply exciting, magical stories.

LEARN MORE! READ THESE ARTICLES…
A GREEK LEGEND: ODYSSEUS AND THE CYCLOPS
A JEWISH LEGEND: THE GOLEM OF PRAGUE
A NIGERIAN FOLKTALE: THE MONKEY COURT

The Bearer of the World

Long, long ago, Zeus, the king of the ancient Greek gods, was very angry with Atlas, one of the Titans (the children of Heaven and Earth). He was angry because Atlas had tried to fight with him. So Zeus ordered Atlas to stand forever holding the heavens and the Earth on his shoulders!

Atlas wanted to get rid of his tiresome job. He almost managed this when the Greek hero Hercules came to ask for his help. Hercules was supposed to get three golden apples that were guarded by a dragon in a garden. Atlas agreed to get the apples if Hercules would hold the heavens and the Earth on his shoulders while he was gone.

When Atlas returned, he told Hercules to keep the job. Hercules agreed. But he asked Atlas to hold the world for just a minute while he found a shoulder-pad for himself. As soon as Atlas lifted the world onto his shoulders, Hercules picked up the golden apples and ran away. Some stories say that thunder is Atlas shouting after Hercules to come back. Most pictures of Atlas show him carrying the world.

This is an ancient Greek story. But today, when we want to learn about the world, we look in a book called an 'atlas'. Here we can see the shapes of countries, the rivers that flow in each country, and where the continents are.

Find and correct the mistakes in the following sentence: Hercules agreed to get three golden apples for Atlas if Atlas would hold the heavens and Earth on his shoulders for a while.

LEARN MORE! READ THESE ARTICLES...
A GREEK LEGEND: ODYSSEUS AND THE CYCLOPS
MYTHS AND LEGENDS, FOLKTALES AND FABLES
THOR: THE THUNDER GOD

DID YOU KNOW?
Atlas is also the name of a range of mountains in north-western Africa. In one story, Atlas was the king of that area. But he was a bad host to the Greek hero Perseus, who showed him the Gorgon's head. Looking at the Gorgon turned men to stone.

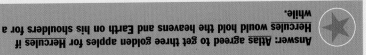

Answer: Atlas agreed to get three golden apples for Hercules if Hercules would hold the heavens and Earth on his shoulders for a while.

9

DID YOU KNOW?
There are some real dragons alive today. They are the giant Komodo dragons, 3-metre-long lizards that live in Indonesia.

SEARCH LIGHT

Which of the following is not breathed out by dragons?
a) ice
b) fire
c) mist

Beasts of Fire and Mist

According to a popular story, there was once a terrible dragon in a city where many people lived. It had huge wings like a bat. The flapping of its wings could be heard for miles. It could kill an ox with a single blow. Its eyes flashed and it breathed fire.

Every year, the people of the city had to offer the dragon a girl to eat, or it would kill everyone. One year it was the turn of Princess Sabra to face the dragon. George, the youngest and bravest of the champions who protected the Christian church, came forward to save her. He wounded the dragon with his magic sword, Ascalon. The princess threw her sash around the dragon's neck and pulled the beast to the marketplace, where George killed it with a single blow. George later became the **patron saint** of England.

People used to believe in all kinds of dragons. The beasts roamed the land, swishing their great scaly tails. They flashed fiery glances from their enormous eyes. They blew rings of poisonous smoke and breathed out flames of fire without ever burning their tongues!

In China and other Asian countries, on the other hand, the dragon, or *long*, is considered good, lucky, and a powerful protector of people. The Chinese emperors adopted the dragon as their symbol. Dragons are linked with water and they breathe out mist and clouds instead of smoke and fire. You can see huge, colourful paper dragons being carried during Chinese New Year and other celebrations. Maybe stories of dragons started because people found dinosaur bones and didn't know what they were. The bones would have looked like they came from monsters.

LEARN MORE! READ THESE ARTICLES…
ATLAS: THE BEARER OF THE WORLD
A KOREAN FOLKTALE: THE TIGER IN THE TRAP
MYTHS AND LEGENDS, FOLKTALES AND FABLES

Who Will Marry Mousie?

SEARCH LIGHT

Who did the father mouse want his daughter to marry?
a) the Sun
b) a mouse
c) the wind

There was once a charming girl mouse who knew everything a young mouse should know. She could gnaw holes, climb high shelves, and squeeze into small spaces.

Her father thought that a smart young mouse would make a fine husband for his daughter. But her mother had other ideas. 'My daughter is finer than anyone in the world. She will not marry a mouse!'

So the three of them went on a journey to the Sun's palace.

'Great Sun,' the mother said. 'Our daughter is so special we want her to marry someone who is greater than all others.'

'I am honoured,' answered the Sun. 'But there is someone greater than I.' As he spoke, a cloud spread itself over the Sun's face.

'I am not really good enough for your daughter,' replied the cloud. 'There is someone more powerful than I.'

As he spoke, the wind swept the cloud across the sky. Now the mother asked the wind to marry her daughter.

But the wind said, 'The wall is greater than I am. He has the power to stop me.'

But the wall said, 'I should not be the husband of such a delightful young girl. It's true that I can stop the wind, which can toss the clouds, which can cover the Sun. But there is someone even greater.'

'Who?' asked the mother.

'A mouse,' said the wall. 'A mouse can pass through me or under me. If you want a son-in-law who is the greatest in all the world, find a mouse.'

So the three mice went home happily, and the daughter married a mouse.

LEARN MORE! READ THESE ARTICLES...

A EUROPEAN FOLKTALE: THE COUNTRY MOUSE AND THE TOWN MOUSE

A STORY FROM JAPAN: THE STONECUTTER

DID YOU KNOW?

There have been many famous mice in children's stories, including Mickey and Minnie Mouse, Mighty Mouse, Speedy Gonzales, Mrs Tittlemouse, Motor Mouse, Danger Mouse, the Tailor of Gloucester, and the Two Bad Mice.

Animal Stories That Teach

Aesop's fables are animal stories that were told in Greece almost 2,500 years ago. They are stories about animals or birds that speak and act like people. Each of these stories tells us a useful truth about everyday life. These truths are called 'morals'.

One of Aesop's fables is about a greedy dog.

A dog had a piece of meat in his mouth and was carrying it home. On the way, the dog looked into a pond and saw his own reflection. It looked like another dog with a second piece of meat. 'Why should *he* eat such good meat?' thought the dog. 'I want that piece too.'

The dog opened his mouth to grab the other piece of meat, and his piece dropped into the water and disappeared. When the greedy dog saw the meat disappear, he put his tail between his legs and crept away.

The moral of this fable is: 'Be careful, or you may lose what you have by grabbing something that isn't there.'

Here is another fable, about a fox.

True or false? The dog lost his meat because he was hungry.

DID YOU KNOW?

The next time someone says something is 'fabulous', you can tell them that the word 'fabulous' comes from the word 'fable'. It means 'amazing' or 'larger-than-life', or even 'imaginary', like a fable.

Strolling through the woods one day, a fox saw a juicy bunch of grapes hanging from a high vine.

'Just the thing for a thirsty fox,' he said to himself.

The fox jumped as high as he could, but he could not reach the grapes. He tried again and again. Each time he just missed the tasty-looking fruit. 'Oh well,' he thought. 'Those grapes are probably sour anyway.' And he went away without the grapes.

The term 'sour grapes' comes from this Aesop's fable about the fox. It refers to the attitude some people show when they sneer at something they can't have.

LEARN MORE! READ THESE ARTICLES…
AN AUSTRALIAN TALE: HOW KANGAROO GOT HIS TAIL
A NATIVE AMERICAN LEGEND: COYOTE BRINGS FIRE
A ZULU STORY: JACKAL GETS AWAY

Answer: FALSE. The dog lost his meat because he was greedy.

The Country Mouse and the Town Mouse

Once, a small grey mouse lived in the country. He had to find food to store for the winter, but when he had stored enough, he thought: 'I'll ask my cousin from town to visit. He might enjoy a holiday.'

At dinner the town mouse asked: 'Is this all you have to eat, a few acorns?'

The country mouse nodded **humbly**.

The next morning the town mouse woke up shivering. 'I was so cold I nearly froze. Come and visit me in town. We'll wine and dine, and I have a nice cosy mouse hole where we can sleep.'

The two set off. It was late when they arrived at the great house. There had been a banquet that day, and the table was still covered with good things to eat.

'Sit down,' invited the town mouse. 'I will bring you some delicious food.'

Then someone opened the door, and in dashed three big dogs, growling and sniffing, and the owners of the house entered.

Two voices shouted: 'Who has been at this table?'

The mice ran all around the room until they found a small hole in a wall where they could hide. Hours later, when the dogs and people finally left the room, the country mouse came out cautiously.

'Thank you for your hospitality, but I like my acorns and my cold winter winds far better than your grand food and warm house. At home, I can sleep in peace and comfort. Here there's always fear to take your appetite away!'

LEARN MORE! READ THESE ARTICLES…
AN ASIAN FOLKTALE: WHO WILL MARRY MOUSIE?
A KOREAN FOLKTALE: THE TIGER IN THE TRAP
A NIGERIAN FOLKTALE: THE MONKEY COURT

DID YOU KNOW?

Real field mice sometimes do move into people's houses to spend the winter and then move back outdoors when the warm weather returns.

SEARCH LIGHT

Did the country mouse get more to eat at his house or at the house of the town mouse?

Answer: The town mouse had more food to choose from, but the country mouse didn't get a chance to eat much of it.

The Golem
of Prague

Many hundreds of years ago there lived many Jewish families in the city of Prague. Although they worked hard, many people in Prague didn't like them. Sometimes Jewish businesses were raided. Sometimes their homes were burned. And sometimes they were killed.

In that time there was a wise rabbi, a great teacher, living in Prague. His name was Rabbi Loew. He knew a way to help his people. He would build a man of clay. He would make the Golem.

Rabbi Loew shaped clay into the form of a man's body. And when he was done, he walked around the clay man seven times, chanting, 'Shanti, Shanti, Dahat, Dahat.' The Golem then opened his eyes and sat up.

'Golem,' said Rabbi Loew. 'I've made you so you can help and protect my people.' The Golem nodded.

'Every day I'll tell you what to do,' continued Rabbi Loew.

At first the Golem was a great gift to the Jewish families of Prague. He helped them in their work and protected them. But the Golem wanted more. So Rabbi Loew taught him to read. But reading about people made him want even more. He wanted to be human.

Rabbi Loew couldn't make the Golem human. The Golem became angry and began to attack the people he had earlier helped. He became a monster.

Rabbi Loew had no choice but to chase the Golem from Prague. No one knows what happened to the Golem. And no one knows where he is today.

LEARN MORE! READ THESE ARTICLES...
DRAGONS: BEASTS OF FIRE AND MIST
A RUSSIAN FOLKTALE: THE BEAR AND THE OLD MAN

DID YOU KNOW?
Modern-day horror films have used the idea of man-made monsters. Perhaps most famous are the various versions of the monster movie *Frankenstein*.

SEARCH LIGHT

The golem
was a
a) clay beast.
b) clay man.
c) clay toy.

Answer: b) clay man.

King Arthur's
Knights of the Round Table

It is said that, long ago, the British people needed a king. One day, the legend goes, a rock appeared with a sword caught in it.

A sign said: 'Whoever Can Pull This Sword from This Rock Will Be Rightful King of the Britons.'

The strongest men in the kingdom tried to pull the sword out of the rock. It would not move. Then along came a young boy called Arthur. He had not heard about the sword in the rock. Thinking he would borrow the sword for his stepbrother, who had gone off to war, Arthur stepped up to the rock. He pulled. The sword slid out easily.

Merlin the magician had placed the sword in the rock. He had kept it there by magic. Only Arthur could remove it. The sword was called Excalibur. Merlin had been Arthur's teacher. He knew that Arthur would be the best king for Britain.

As king, Arthur needed people to help him rule wisely. He decided he would ask the strongest and bravest men to help him. He sent messengers to look for these strong and brave men.

Many men came to help Arthur. He asked them to promise to be fair, to keep their word and to protect the weak. They became Arthur's Knights of the Round Table. Lancelot would become the greatest of all the Knights of the Round Table. But Arthur made the table round for a reason. It meant that everyone seated was equal there, and no one could sit at the 'head' of the table.

King Arthur's legend also says that if Britain is ever in danger, he will come back and save the people once again.

LEARN MORE! READ THESE ARTICLES…
A GREEK LEGEND: ODYSSEUS AND THE CYCLOPS
MYTHS AND LEGENDS, FOLKTALES AND FABLES

SEARCH LIGHT

Find and correct the mistake in the following sentence: The name of Arthur's famous sword was Lancelot.

DID YOU KNOW?

Although the Arthur story is a legend, there might really have been a 6th-century military leader who led the British against invaders.

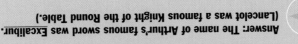

Answer: The name of Arthur's famous sword was Excalibur. (Lancelot was a famous Knight of the Round Table.)

SEARCH LIGHT

How many eyes does the Cyclops have?
a) a million
b) ten
c) one

DID YOU KNOW?
Some scientists think the legend of Cyclops might have developed when people found elephant bones and didn't know what they were. The elephant skull has a large hole that looks like a single eye socket.

Odysseus and the Cyclops

Long ago, the Greek king Odysseus was sailing home from war with his men. Along the way, they stopped at an island where one-eyed man-eating giants called Cyclopes lived.

Odysseus and his men wandered into a cave belonging to the Cyclops Polyphemus. At **twilight** Polyphemus returned with his flocks of sheep. When Polyphemus and all the sheep were inside, he picked up a huge stone and closed the mouth of the cave. Odysseus and his men were trapped!

Polyphemus ate up two of Odysseus' men and fell fast asleep. In the morning he ate two more men and, after blocking the mouth of the cave, went off with his sheep. The stone was too heavy for the men to move. Odysseus, however, thought of a plan. He sharpened the branch of an olive tree.

When Polyphemus came home that night, Odysseus offered him wine. The Cyclops drank it and asked Odysseus' name.

Odysseus answered, 'People call me Nobody.'

'Your gift, Nobody, is that I shall eat you last,' said Polyphemus. And, drunk with wine, he fell fast asleep.

Odysseus then took the great sharp branch and drove it into the sleeping giant's eye, blinding him. When Polyphemus cried out for help, the other Cyclopes shouted, 'Who is hurting you?'

'Nobody,' screamed Polyphemus.

'Well, then you don't need any help from us,' said the other giants.

Meanwhile, Odysseus and each of his men **lashed** together three sheep. Under the middle sheep, each man clung to the **fleece**. Finally everybody was hidden.

Polyphemus did not think of feeling under the bellies of the sheep. And so the men escaped to their ship and continued their long journey home.

LEARN MORE! READ THESE ARTICLES...
ATLAS: THE BEARER OF THE WORLD
PAUL BUNYAN: THE TALE OF A LUMBERJACK

The Trojan Horse

More than 3,000 years ago the Greeks and the Trojans fought a long and terrible war. For about ten years the Greek army camped outside the city of Troy. The strong wall around the city stopped them from getting in.

There were many battles during these years. The Greek soldiers tried to knock down the wall. They couldn't. They tried to climb over it, but the Trojans always pushed them away. Then the Greeks thought of a trick. They started building a very big horse made of wood.

Watching this, the Trojans were puzzled. They were even more puzzled one morning when they saw that the Greek army had gone away. Only the strange wooden horse was standing outside their gates.

The Trojans went out to look at it. They liked the beautiful wooden horse so they pulled it inside the walls. They thought the war was over because the Greeks had left. They put away their swords and spears. They sang and danced around the horse.

Finally, the Trojans went to sleep. Then the Greeks played their trick. Greek soldiers had hidden inside the hollow wooden horse. That night, they climbed out of the horse and opened the gates of Troy to all the other Greek soldiers.

The Greeks caught the Trojans completely by surprise and captured the city of Troy. Even today, we often call a tricky inside attack a 'Trojan horse'.

LEARN MORE! READ THESE ARTICLES...
A GREEK LEGEND: ODYSSEUS AND THE CYCLOPS
A SOUTH ASIAN TALE: THE MONKEY AND THE STRING OF PEARLS

Answer: The Greeks built a large wooden horse to trick the Trojans.

The Thunder God

Long ago, in Europe's northern lands of ice and snow, most people believed that Thor was king of all the gods. Thor was the mighty god of thunder and the sky. He was the eldest son of Odin. Thursday, the fifth day of the week, is named after him (Thor's day).

Thor had a red beard and was very tall and strong. He had a magic belt that made him doubly strong whenever he wore it. He used his strength to protect people from giants and evil fairies.

His hammer, called Mjollnir, was his main weapon and produced lightning bolts. Thor had to wear special iron gloves to hold it. It would always return to him after killing the person it was thrown at. It could split a mountain in half or kill all the frost giants in one blow.

Thor travelled in a **chariot** that was drawn by two goats. One of them was called Tooth-Gnasher and the other was Tooth-Grinder. Whenever it moved across the sky, the chariot produced thunder, and glowing sparks flew from its wheels.

Soldiers worshiped Thor because of his strength. Peasants and farmers worshiped him because he made the rain for their crops.

LEARN MORE! READ THESE ARTICLES...
ATLAS: THE BEARER OF THE WORLD
A CAMBODIAN MYTH: MONI MEKHALA AND REAM EYSO

SEARCH LIGHT

Which day of the week is named for Thor?

DID YOU KNOW?

Thor's qualities may sound like some fictional superheroes you've heard of before. In fact, Thor himself has appeared as a comic book superhero.

Answer: Thursday (Thor's day) is named for the Norse god.

The Bear and the Old Man

There was a time when bears and people got along well together. One day an old man was out planting turnips in a field near his house. As he was working, a bear came out of the woods.

'What are you doing in my field, Old Man?' asked the bear.

'I'm planting turnips,' he replied. 'Do you mind if I use your field, Bear?'

'No,' said the bear. 'Just share the turnips with me when you are done.'

When it came time to harvest the turnips, the bear asked, 'Where's my share, Old Man?'

'I've decided to split them with you, half and half,' said the old man. 'You can have the tops, Bear, and I'll keep the roots.'

This sounded fair, but when the bear ate the green turnip tops, he found them **bitter**. He realized he'd been tricked - for turnip roots were sweet.

SEARCH LIGHT

Find and correct the mistake in the following sentence: The bear didn't like turnip tops because they tasted sour.

The next year, the old man was again in the field.

'Old Man,' he said. 'You tricked me last year. I want my fair share this year, and this time I want the roots.'

'Okay, Bear,' said the old man. 'This year I'm planting rye. When it's grown you shall have the roots and I'll take the tops.'

The bear was pleased with himself, thinking he had made a good deal. But rye is a grain, and the food is at the top of its stems. When he tried eating the rye roots, he discovered that they had no taste. He realized that he been tricked once again. And ever since, bears and people have not got along.

LEARN MORE! READ THESE ARTICLES…
A KOREAN FOLKTALE: THE TIGER IN THE TRAP
A NIGERIAN FOLKTALE: THE MONKEY COURT

DID YOU KNOW?
Many people enjoy eating cooked turnip tops, also called 'turnip greens'. They become less bitter, but still taste interesting.

Answer: The bear didn't like turnip tops because they tasted bitter.

29

Yeh-Shen

Once there was a man with a beautiful daughter called Yeh-Shen. **Alas**, before the girl grew up, her father died. So Yeh-Shen was brought up by her stepmother.

Now the stepmother already had a daughter of her own. So the stepmother gave Yeh-Shen all the hardest jobs. Yeh-Shen had no friends other than a golden fish, a carp. Yeh-Shen always shared what she had with her friend the carp.

One day the stepmother discovered Yeh-Shen's secret friend. She caught the fish and cooked it for breakfast. As Yeh-Shen gathered up the bones of the fish, the skeleton told her that it could grant wishes.

Yeh-Shen was eager to go to the Spring Festival. But Yeh-Shen's stepmother refused to let her go. She was afraid that pretty Yeh-Shen would get all the attention and her own daughter would get none. So Yeh-Shen asked the bones for help. As soon as she said the words, she was dressed in a gown of peacock feathers. On her feet were beautiful golden slippers.

At the festival Yeh-Shen danced and danced and had a wonderful time. But when she saw her stepmother approaching, she was frightened and ran away, leaving behind one golden slipper.

The next morning everyone was talking about the beautiful stranger.

SEARCH LIGHT

Fill in the gaps: Instead of a fairy godmother, such as Cinderella had, Yeh-Shen had a _____ to help her.

DID YOU KNOW?
A 9th-century-AD Chinese version of this classic story is one of the earliest known. There are about 300 different variations of the Cinderella story.

The **magistrate** announced that his son wanted to marry the woman whose foot fitted the slipper. But though many tried, no one's foot would fit.

When the magistrate saw Yeh-Shen, he asked her to try on the slipper. The slipper fitted perfectly. Yeh-Shen and the magistrate's son were married and lived happily together all their lives.

LEARN MORE! READ THESE ARTICLES...
AN ASIAN FOLKTALE: WHO WILL MARRY MOUSIE?
A STORY FROM JAPAN: THE STONECUTTER

Answer: Instead of a fairy godmother, such as Cinderella had, Yeh-Shen had a magic skeleton (or fish skeleton) to help her.

31

The Stonecutter

There was once a poor stonecutter who went daily to the mountain near his house and cut stone to use in building houses. One morning he saw a palace being built and immediately realized how **humble** his life was.

'Oh, if only I could have that palace, then I would truly be happy.'

And suddenly it was true. Unknown to the stonecutter, the spirit of the mountain had granted his wish. The stonecutter was happy, but soon he realized that even princes get hot in the Sun.

'Oh, if only I could be like the Sun, then I would truly be happy.' And suddenly it was true.

The stonecutter was again very happy. But one day a cloud drifted in front of him and blocked all his glorious rays.

'Oh, if only I could be like this cloud, then I would truly be happy.' And suddenly it was true.

But he grew tired of being a cloud, for every day the wind blew him around.

'Oh, if only I could be like the wind, then I would truly be happy.' And suddenly it was true.

One day he ran into the mountain, which wouldn't move no matter how hard he blew.

'Oh, if only I could be like the mountain, then I would truly be happy.' And suddenly it was true.

But a tiny itch bothered him. When he looked down, he saw a stonecutter chipping away pieces of stone.

Then he knew where happiness lay. 'Oh, if only I could be a stonecutter, then I would be content for the rest of my life.' And suddenly it was true.

And he was finally truly happy.

LEARN MORE! READ THESE ARTICLES...
AN ASIAN FOLKTALE: WHO WILL MARRY MOUSIE?
A STORY FROM GHANA: ANANSE AND THE WISDOM POT

SEARCH LIGHT

Put these in the order they occur in the story: mountain, Sun, prince, cloud, stonecutter, stonecutter, wind

DID YOU KNOW?
Stonecutters may have lived simple lives, but they have contributed to some very grand structures. For example, stonecutters played a major role in building the Great Pyramids of Egypt.

Why did
the tiger
want to eat
the man?

The Tiger in the Trap

Once there was a traveller. He was just getting ready to stop for the night when he heard a low moaning. He found a tiger trapped in a deep pit.

The tiger saw the man and begged, 'Please free me from this trap, and I will be grateful to you for the rest of my life.'

The traveller agreed and lowered a large branch into the pit for the tiger to climb out. As soon as the tiger was free, he fell upon the man.

'Wait!' said the traveller. 'I thought you were going to be grateful to me.'

'It was men who trapped me,' answered the tiger. 'So a man should suffer for it.'

Just then a **hare** hopped by and asked what was happening. The tiger explained and then asked if the hare agreed with him.

'First I have to see the pit. Where were you?' the hare asked the tiger.

'Down here,' the tiger replied and jumped into the pit.

'Was the branch there too?' asked the hare.

'No,' said the tiger. And so the hare took the branch away.

Then the hare turned to the traveller and told him to be on his way.

The tiger cried out in **dismay** as the man walked off down the trail. 'How could you betray me?'

'I judge each according to his own and not by his fellows,' answered the hare. 'You have the fate you deserve and so does the man.'

Learn More! Read these articles…
A Chinese Cinderella Story: Yeh-Shen
A Nigerian Folktale: The Monkey Court

Answer: Other men had trapped the tiger so the tiger thought this man should pay for it.

The Monkey
and the
String of Pearls

SEARCH LIGHT

Fill in
the gap:
The first monkey
stole the pearls
so she could look
_____.

One of the most popular kinds of stories in South Asia are called Jataka tales. They tell about the past lives of the Buddha, in both human and animal form. Similar South Asian tales occur in Hindu and other non-Buddhist literature. All these stories aim to teach a lesson, as does this one.

The king and queen decided to have a swim one beautiful day. The queen did not want to lose her jewellery so she took off her pearls and gave them to a handmaid. The handmaid soon grew tired in the warm sun and fell asleep.

A monkey had been watching and quickly ran down the tree, snatched the necklace, and raced back up into the branches. The monkey thought she looked **regal** in the pearls. 'Aren't I beautiful?' she said to herself.

When the maid awoke she noticed that the pearls were missing. 'The queen's necklace has been stolen!' she cried. But no matter how hard the king's guards looked, they couldn't find the thief. The captain of the guards was puzzled. He decided to put out glass necklaces in the hope of catching his thief.

When the other monkeys saw the many glass necklaces lying on the ground, they quickly snatched them up and chattered happily to themselves, 'Oh, don't we look stunning?'

All except the first monkey. She reached into her hiding place for the string of pearls and put it on. 'Your necklaces are just glass,' she teased, 'but mine is made of pearls.'

This was what the captain of the guards had been waiting for, and he and his men sprang from their hiding places and caught the monkey. They returned the string of pearls to their queen and let the rest of the monkeys keep the glass necklaces.

LEARN MORE! READ THESE ARTICLES...
FROM THE *KALILAH WA DIMNAH*: THE POOR MAN AND THE FLASK OF OIL
A NIGERIAN FOLKTALE: THE MONKEY COURT

DID YOU KNOW?
Some animals really do like jewellery. Birds such as magpies often steal and collect shiny things like aluminium foil or silver chain.

Answer: The first monkey stole the pearls so she could look regal.

The Poor Man
and the Flask of Oil

About the 8th century, the writer Ibn al-Muqaffa made a famous Arabic translation of the South Asian stories known as tales of Bidpai. The translation was called the *Kalilah wa Dimnah* (after the two jackals in the book's first story, Kalilah and Dimnah). It provided a treasure of tales and parables that would appear throughout Islamic literature. This is one of those well-known tales.

A poor man lived next to a rich man who sold oil for a living. The poor man envied his neighbour's wealth and riches and often talked about them. So the rich man gave the poor man a **flask** of oil as a gift.

The poor man was delighted. 'I could sell the oil,' thought the poor man. 'Then I would have enough money to buy five goats.'

Later he thought some more. 'With five goats,' he said to himself, 'a man would be rich enough to have a wife.' He liked this thought so much he added to it. 'Of course, my wife would be beautiful and give me a fine son.'

But then the poor man had a thought that worried him. 'What if my son is lazy because his father is a wealthy man? What if he refuses to obey me and disgraces me?'

This thought made the poor man so angry that he began stomping around his hut, swinging his staff. 'Why, if my son refuses to obey me, then I'll teach him a lesson. I'll beat him with my **staff**.'

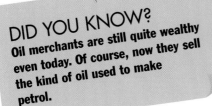

SEARCH LIGHT

Why, in the olden days, would a man who sold oil be wealthy?

As the staff swung about, it nudged the flask of oil off its shelf. The flask crashed to the ground and broke, spilling its contents on the dirt. The man looked at the shards of the flask, realizing that his dreams were now just as broken. And once more he was just a poor man living next to a wealthy neighbour.

LEARN MORE! READ THESE ARTICLES...
A EUROPEAN FOLKTALE:
THE COUNTRY MOUSE AND THE
TOWN MOUSE
A SOUTH ASIAN TALE:
THE MONKEY AND THE STRING
OF PEARLS

Answer: Oil has long been used as a fuel for lamps and was very valuable when there wasn't yet any electricity.

39

Moni Mekhala
and Ream Eyso

At one time, both the goddess Moni Mekhala and the giant Ream Eyso were studying with the same teacher. This teacher was very wise.

After a few years of teaching them both, the wise teacher decided to hold a contest for her students. She asked them to bring her a full glass of dew the next morning. Whoever brought her a glass full of dew first would win a prize, a magic ball.

Both got up very early and went to gather their glasses of dew.

Ream Eyso was quite pleased with himself. 'Surely my idea of pouring the dew off the leaves is brilliant,' he said.

Moni Mekhala had actually started the night before by laying a scarf on the grass. 'This worked beautifully,' she said as she wrung the scarf out into a cup.

The goddess won the magic ball, and the giant was given a magic axe as a second prize. Ream Eyso was jealous of Moni Mekhala. So he took his axe and threw it at the goddess. It made a terrible rumble as it flew through the air.

Moni Mekhala heard the noise and held up her magic ball. She caused the ball to strike the giant with great, jagged sparks of fire. The fire made him so hot that he dripped large drops of sweat all over the ground.

Even today you can hear the rumble and see the sparks as Ream Eyso's sweat falls to the ground.

LEARN MORE! READ THESE ARTICLES…
MYTHS AND LEGENDS, FOLKTALES AND FABLES
THOR

SEARCH LIGHT

What natural occurrence does this story explain?

40

DID YOU KNOW?
In North American Indian mythology, a spirit called the Thunderbird watered the Earth. Lightning was believed to flash from its beak, and rolling thunder came from the beating of its wings.

Answer: This story explains the source of thunder, lightning, and rain.

41

How Kangaroo
Got His Tail

SEARCH LIGHT

Match up the animals with their descriptions.

Kangaroo Wombat
sleeps outside
sleeps in a hole
flat head
long tail

Long ago, before kangaroos had long tails and before wombats had flat heads, the animals played and lived together. Kangaroo and Wombat were great friends and spent every day together. But at night, each one liked to sleep in a different way. Wombat liked to sleep indoors, warm and snug. Kangaroo liked to sleep outdoors, beneath the stars. Each thought his way of sleeping was the best.

Then, one night, a terrible storm cracked open the sky, and harsh winds and rain **scoured** the land. Kangaroo was outside and was miserable in the cold, wet night. He knocked on Wombat's house and called to Wombat to let him come in to warm up. But Wombat thought about the amount of space Kangaroo would take up, so he refused to let him in.

Kangaroo was very angry about being locked out in the storm. He picked up a big rock and dropped it through the roof of Wombat's house.

'There,' Kangaroo shouted. 'Now your house will be damp all the time.'

The rock landed on Wombat's head and flattened his brow. Wombat grabbed a spear and threw it as hard as he could at Kangaroo. The spear pierced the end of Kangaroo's tail.

No matter how hard Kangaroo pulled, the spear wouldn't come out, and his tail just stretched longer and longer.

Since that day, Kangaroo and Wombat have not been friends. Kangaroo still has a big tail and sleeps outside. And Wombat still has a flat head and sleeps in a hole.

LEARN MORE! READ THESE ARTICLES…
A CHEROKEE STORY: WHY POSSUM'S TAIL IS BARE
A RUSSIAN FOLKTALE: THE BEAR AND THE OLD MAN

Answer: Kangaroo: sleeps outside, long tail
Wombat: sleeps in a hole, flat head

Who is Ntikume?

DID YOU KNOW?
The West African character Ananse (or Anansi) also appears in Jamaican tales. This shows how folktales travelled from Africa with the slave trade to the West Indies.

Ananse
and the Wisdom Pot

Ananse the spider was far and wide considered to be the wisest of all animals, and many animals came to him with their problems and questions.

After a while, Ananse grew tired of answering so many questions and decided he would have to do something to regain his peace and quiet. So he put all of his wisdom into a giant pot. He strapped the pot to his belly. He planned to carry the pot to a branch of a tall tree where all the animals could go to get their own answers to their questions.

But as he was climbing the tree, the pot kept getting in the way of his legs and slowed him down. Ntikume, one of Ananse's many sons, saw this. He suggested that Ananse strap the pot to his back instead, where it wouldn't be in his way.

When Ananse heard this he was furious. He couldn't **tolerate** the thought that his son should have a better idea than his own. So Ananse grabbed the pot and flung it to the ground, where it shattered into a thousand pieces.

Ever since then, wisdom has been scattered all over the world for many people to find.

LEARN MORE! READ THESE ARTICLES…
AESOP'S FABLES: ANIMAL STORIES THAT TEACH
A FABLE OF THE PACIFIC NORTHWEST: RAVEN AND CROW'S POTLATCH
A ZULU STORY: JACKAL GETS AWAY

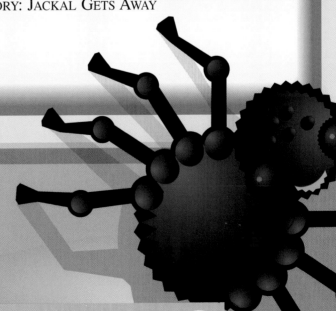

Answer: Ntikume is one of Ananse's many sons.

The Monkey Court

Once two young friends were walking along together when they saw a large piece of meat. Each boy thought he had seen the meat first, so each thought he deserved to have it. The two argued over the meat. And though they both thought it right to share, they thought that the other should take the smaller portion. They agreed to take their **dispute** to the Monkey Court.

Now Monkey saw them coming and he realized that here was a real chance for him. So he put on his wisest face and listened patiently to their story. When the two boys had finished talking, Monkey said, 'I shall divide the meat equally between you.' With that, Monkey tore the meat in two and was about to hand it over when he noticed that the two pieces were uneven.

SEARCH LIGHT

Why do you think the two boys expected Monkey to solve problems for them?

'I will fix this so that each of you gets the same amount of meat,' said Monkey. And with that he took a bite from the larger piece of meat. But once more he noticed that the two pieces were uneven. And no matter how carefully Monkey bit the pieces of meat, one piece always ended up being bigger. Finally there were only two small pieces of meat.

At that point Monkey said, 'It is time for me to take my fee for being your judge. These two tiny pieces of meat will do just fine.' And with that he sent the two hungry, and wiser, boys on their way.

LEARN MORE! READ THESE ARTICLES…
AN ASIAN FOLKTALE: WHO WILL MARRY MOUSIE?
A FABLE OF THE PACIFIC NORTHWEST: RAVEN AND CROW'S POTLATCH

DID YOU KNOW?
In many African tales, the monkey and several other animals are clever and the human beings are usually shown to be foolish.

Answer: Monkey had a reputation for being clever, as you see from the story. So the boys expected that he could solve their problems. But instead, he outsmarted them whilst teaching them a lesson about being greedy.

Jackal Gets Away

Jackal was known for his cleverness and often used his wits to trick other animals. He especially enjoyed playing tricks on mighty Lion. But one day Lion almost put an end to all of Jackal's pranks.

Jackal was walking along, feeling **smug** while thinking about how he had just tricked Hyena out of a meal. He was not paying attention to where he was going, and instead he was laughing about how clever he was.

Only when it was too late did Jackal realize that he had walked right into Lion's **territory**. He was about to turn and run when he saw Lion just a few steps away. Lion was staring at him, and not looking at all friendly. Jackal knew he was in serious trouble for he could never hope to outrun Lion when he was this close.

But Jackal didn't panic. Instead he started wailing out loud and digging at the ground. 'Oh, Lion. What will

DID YOU KNOW?

Like many African trickster characters, Jackal is a clever underdog figure, smaller and weaker than his rival. Jackal's target - Lion in this story - is usually sincere, hardworking, and slow-witted.

SEARCH LIGHT

Why do you
think Jackal
was afraid
of Lion?

we do? Those rocks over there are falling and they'll surely crush us both.'

Lion quickly looked at the rocks, and indeed they did seem to be tilting in a frightening way. He had never paid much attention to them before. He didn't realize that this was how they always looked.

'Quick, Lion,' cried Jackal, 'use your mighty strength to stop the rocks while I go find a log to prop them up.'

Lion threw his huge shoulder against the rocks and pushed with all his might.

We'll never know how long he stayed there before he realized that Jackal had tricked him once again. Perhaps he's still there.

LEARN MORE! READ THESE ARTICLES...
AESOP'S FABLES: ANIMAL STORIES THAT TEACH
A NATIVE AMERICAN LEGEND: COYOTE
BRINGS FIRE

Answer: Not only might lions eat jackals, but lions don't like other predators to be in their territory.

Rabbit Throws Away His Sandal

Rabbit was the wisest of all the animals, and so he was their mayor. Although he was a good leader, he wasn't well liked because he used his wits to play tricks on the other animals.

One morning all the animals decided they would get rid of Rabbit and his tricks. They gathered outside of Rabbit's burrow, planning to grab him and tear him to pieces as soon as he came out.

But Rabbit heard them grumbling. He called back, 'I'll be out as soon as I find my sandals.'

It was still dark as the Sun had yet to rise. The animals all began to shout, 'Rabbit, hurry up. We need your help.'

Rabbit called back, 'I've found one sandal, but it's broken and it'll take time to fix it.'

DID YOU KNOW?
Rabbits appear in the folktales of several different cultures. For instance the Brer ('Brother') Rabbit of African American tales grew out of an African character, Hare. Both are clever, like Rabbit in this Mayan story from Central America.

SEARCH LIGHT

Which animal is not in the story?
a) dog
b) skunk
c) snake

Jaguar, who was quite impatient, said, 'Throw it out here and I'll fix it while you look for the other sandal.'

Jaguar grabbed the object that flew out of the burrow and tossed it into bushes.

After a while, Skunk said, 'What's keeping you, Rabbit?' But no one answered.

Then Vulture said, 'Snake, slither into that hole and see what's keeping Rabbit.'

Snake did just that. But he could see very quickly that he was alone in the burrow. 'There's no one here. Rabbit's disappeared.'

Then from the bushes everyone heard Rabbit laugh. They realized he had tricked them once again. They had been so eager waiting for Rabbit that no one noticed he had thrown himself out instead of his sandal.

LEARN MORE! READ THESE ARTICLES...
AESOP'S FABLES: ANIMAL STORIES THAT TEACH
A ZULU STORY: JACKAL GETS AWAY

SEARCH LIGHT

True or false?
Paul Bunyan
was a real man.

DID YOU KNOW?
The legend of Paul Bunyan may have come from stories that real lumberjacks told around the fire on cold evenings.

The Tale of a Lumberjack

If somebody told you that a giant woodsman had created a 160 kilometre-long inlet to float logs to a mill, would you believe it? Probably not, but it makes a good story.

Stories like that are called 'tall tales', and an imaginary giant lumberjack named Paul Bunyan figures in many American tall tales. A lumberjack is a man who earns his living by cutting down trees. Paul was so big and powerful that he could make hills, lakes, and rivers whenever he wanted to. In fact, he's supposed to have created the Grand Canyon and the Great Lakes.

Paul Bunyan was so big that when he sneezed, a whole hillside of pine trees would fall over. Being such a large man, Paul would get very hungry. He was especially fond of pancakes. The frying pan for making them was so big that people would skate around it with slabs of bacon tied to their feet to grease it.

Paul had a famous helper that he found during the 'blue winter'. People called it the 'blue winter' because the snow that fell was all blue! One night Paul heard an animal crying. When he looked outside, he saw a pair of silky blue ears sticking out of the snow. Paul pulled and pulled. Out of the blue snow came a baby blue ox!

Paul took the ox home with him and named it Babe. When Babe grew up, he was nearly as big as a small mountain.

One story tells of a road with so many curves in it that people didn't know whether they were coming or going. Paul laughed and picked up one end of the road and tied it to Babe. Babe tugged and pulled all the curves out of the road.

LEARN MORE! READ THESE ARTICLES…
ATLAS: THE BEARER OF THE WORLD
A CAMBODIAN MYTH: MONI MEKHALA AND REAM EYSO

Answer: FALSE. As far as anyone knows there never was an actual lumberjack named Paul Bunyan.

How Crow Brought Daylight to the World

There was a time when the world of the north was always in darkness. The people wished for light and Crow told them he had seen daylight on one of his many travels.

'Please bring us some daylight,' the people begged Crow.

Crow flew for many miles. Just when he thought he couldn't fly any more, he saw daylight ahead of him.

When he reached daylight, he landed in a tree to rest. While Crow was resting, the chief's daughter came along. Crow turned himself into a speck of dust and landed on the girl's **parka**. Then Crow heard a baby crying.

'What's wrong?' the girl asked her young brother.

Crow drifted into the baby's ear and whispered: 'Tell her you want a ball of daylight to play with.'

The chief's daughter tied a piece of string to a ball of daylight and gave it to her brother to play with. When the girl carried her brother and the ball of daylight outside, Crow turned back into a bird, grabbed the ball by its string and flew away.

When he arrived home, the people were overjoyed. 'We have daylight!' they cheered. 'We can see the whole world.'

But Crow warned them: 'It is just a small ball of daylight. It will need to rest every now and then, so you won't have daylight for the whole year.'

And that is why the people of the frozen north have half a year of daylight and half a year of darkness.

LEARN MORE! READ THESE ARTICLES…
A CAMBODIAN MYTH: MONI MEKHALA AND REAM EYSO
A FABLE OF THE PACIFIC NORTHWEST: RAVEN AND CROW'S
POTLATCH

SEARCH LIGHT

Fill in the gap: This story explains why there is daylight for only _____ the year in the far north.

DID YOU KNOW?
Crow is a popular figure because of his wisdom. He appears in many Native American myths.

Coyote Brings Fire

Many long years ago fire belonged only to the Fire People. This was a problem for the Animal People during the winter when the winds blew cold. So one year the animals got together to talk about their problem.

'If we don't have fire this winter, then many of our aged grandparents will die,' said Squirrel. 'Let's ask Coyote what we should do. He's clever and always has a plan.'

Coyote listened to the other animals and then told them he had an idea. He told the other animals to be ready to make a great noise when he swished his tail. Coyote led them up into the hills where the Fire People lived. Alone, Coyote dragged himself into the firelight of the Fire People's camp.

'Who's there?' growled one of the Fire People. And then, 'No fear, it's just sorry Coyote.'

As soon as everything was quiet, Coyote swished his tail. At once a great wailing arose all around the camp.

The Fire People jumped up thinking they were being attacked. Coyote then grabbed a piece of fire with his mouth and bounded off down the hill. One of the Fire People reached out and grabbed Coyote's tail, **scorching** it white.

Coyote tossed the fire to Squirrel, who was waiting. The Fire People almost caught Squirrel. The heat from their bodies was so strong that it curled Squirrel's tail. But Squirrel quickly passed the fire to Wood, who swallowed it. Try as they might, the Fire People couldn't make Wood spit out the fire.

Later, Coyote showed the other animals how, whenever they wanted fire, all they had to do was rub two sticks together and Wood would release the fire for them.

LEARN MORE! READ THESE ARTICLES...
A FABLE OF THE PACIFIC NORTHWEST: RAVEN AND CROW'S POTLATCH
A ZULU STORY: JACKAL GETS AWAY

SEARCH LIGHT

The animals wanted fire because
a) they wanted to cook.
b) they wanted to stay warm.
c) they were jealous.

DID YOU KNOW?

Coyote, like several other animals in folktales of different cultures, is a 'trickster' character. Tricksters are often heroes, are usually smart, are sometimes magical, and often get tripped up by their own pride.

Answer: b) they wanted to stay warm.

Why Possum's Tail Is Bare

Possum once had a bushy tail covered with thick, glossy fur. In conversation, he always managed to mention his tail: 'When I was brushing my beautiful tail yesterday, you'll never guess what I saw...'

The other animals were tired of hearing about Possum's tail. But Rabbit said: 'Don't worry, I have a plan.'

The next day Rabbit announced that there was going to be a grand dance. 'We'll want to do something special with your tail,' he said to Possum.

'First,' said Rabbit, 'we need to wash and comb your tail.'

So they dipped Possum's tail in the river, and then Rabbit pulled a pine cone through Possum's tail fur.

'Ouch!' cried Possum. 'You're hurting me.'

'I can stop if you want me to,' replied Rabbit.

'No, no,' said Possum. 'Keep working on my tail.'

So Rabbit kept pulling the pine cone sharply over Possum's tail.

'Now we'll just wrap your tail in this red ribbon,' Rabbit told him.

SEARCH LIGHT

This story
explains
why possums
a) play dead.
b) climb trees.
c) carry their babies.

Possum was so excited. As soon as he reached the dance, he untied the ribbon. And as he did so, all the other animals started to laugh.

'What's so funny?' shouted Possum. Then he looked at his tail. It was as bare and smooth as Snake's back. Rabbit had pulled all the fur off Possum's tail!

'Oh, oh!' wailed Possum and fainted on his back.

And that's why, when you see Possum today, his tail is bare, and if you scare him he rolls over onto his back.

LEARN MORE! READ THESE ARTICLES…
AN AUSTRALIAN TALE: HOW KANGAROO GOT HIS TAIL
A NATIVE AMERICAN LEGEND: COYOTE BRINGS FIRE

DID YOU KNOW?
'Possum' is a shortened form of 'opossum', the full name of this American animal. It's a member of the marsupial family, as are the kangaroos and koalas of Australia.

Raven and Crow's Potlatch

Raven was a crafty fellow, always playing tricks. All during the autumn he teased the other animals as they gathered food. When winter came Raven realized what a fool he'd been. He was cold and hungry.

So Raven went to see Squirrel. 'Friend,' he called. 'Won't you share some of your food?'

'No!' said Squirrel. 'You made fun of me, and now you can starve.'

Disappointed, Raven went to see Bear. 'Friend Bear,' called Raven. 'Won't you share some food with your poor friend Raven?'

But Bear was asleep, and he'd eaten all his food before settling in for his winter sleep.

Raven was hungrier than ever. He thought hard and decided to visit his cousin Crow. 'Why Crow, aren't you ready?' he asked.

'Ready for what?' Crow asked.

'Your **potlatch** feast. All the animals will be here soon. They can't wait to hear you sing.'

Now Crow was vain about his voice, so he was very excited.

Raven went out and invited all the animals to the potlatch. 'Come to my potlatch. There'll be mountains of food.'

Soon all the animals had gathered, and they began to stuff themselves with Crow's food. Crow sang until all he could do was croak. By the time he had finished, Crow was hungry. He wasn't worried, though, because every guest at a potlatch has to invite the host to a thank-you feast.

But while he waited all winter long, Crow was never invited to any feasts. All the animals thought that the potlatch had been Raven's, so Raven was treated to feasts. And Crow has never stopped being hungry. You can still see him today wherever people are, begging for food in his harsh, croaking voice.

LEARN MORE! READ THESE ARTICLES…
AN INUIT TALE: HOW CROW BROUGHT DAYLIGHT TO THE WORLD
A STORY FROM ANCIENT GREECE: THE TROJAN HORSE

DID YOU KNOW?
This story may have developed or at least changed after Pacific American Indians came into contact with white traders. In earlier Indian traditions, guests at potlatch feasts were not expected to invite the host to a feast in return.

SEARCH LIGHT

Fill in the gaps: Before tricking Crow, Raven asks _____ and _____ for help.

Answer: Before tricking Crow, Raven asks Squirrel and Bear for help.

G L O S S A R Y

alas unfortunately or sadly

bitter taste that is sharp and harsh, like a fruit that is not ripe

chariot ancient two-wheeled battle cart pulled by horses

dismay sadness or disappointment

dispute to argue with

flask container for liquid

fleece wool of an animal such as a sheep or a goat

hare rabbit-like animal

humble poor or meek

lash to tie or attach

magistrate official who looks after the laws of a particular area

parka hooded heavy jacket for very cold weather

patron saint holy person who is chosen to specially protect a group or place

potlatch in the American Pacific Northwest, traditional American Indian feast where the host gives out many gifts to show wealth and generosity

regal royal or noble

scorch to burn a surface, usually changing its colour

scour to scrub hard

smug conceited; full of oneself; self-satisfied

staff wooden walking stick

territory area, especially an area claimed by an animal

tolerate to put up with

twilight the light between the end of day and the beginning of night; also, the name for that time of day